The Bird in the Plum Tree

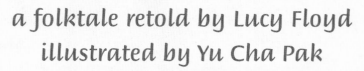

a folktale retold by Lucy Floyd
illustrated by Yu Cha Pak

Harcourt

Orlando   Boston   Dallas   Chicago   San Diego

Visit *The Learning Site!*

www.harcourtschool.com

There was once a great leader
called Mighty One. He loved
plum trees. He loved the light,
beautiful look of them.

Then a tree died. "What a
shame!" he thought. "I wonder
if we might find another one."

Nearby, an artist and his family owned a plum tree. The boy, little Tim-Tim, had a friend who lived in the tree.

4

As the light faded every night,
Tim-Tim went to see his special
friend.

Under the bright stars, Tim-Tim
said, "Night bird, night bird,
sing your bright song.
Sing your bright, bright song!"

Mighty One sent men to look for
a plum tree. "This is the right
one," they said. "It's light. We'll
move it right now."

"I am afraid there's nothing we can do," the artist said to Tim-Tim. "It's for Mighty One. But this might help you picture the tree."

8

"I wonder what might happen
if I tied a note to the tree,"
Tim-Tim thought.

Tim-Tim cried as his night bird
flew away, following the tree. "If
only I could join you, night bird!"
he sighed.

10

Mighty One thought his new tree
was wonderful. Then he saw the
note tied tight to a branch.

"What a special picture of my beautiful tree!" Mighty One said. "It's just right!"

12

He saw a verse also.

My night bird sang songs
High up in the plum tree.
Now he sings no more for me.

Mighty One thought about
the note. He sent for Tim-Tim
right away.

"You lost your friend because of me," Mighty One said to Tim-Tim. "That isn't right. I want to give the tree back to you."

"I want only this picture, Tim-Tim.
I want others to know that I can
learn much from a little one."

16